Bill Easterly
1-19-99

PRIZE IN THE SNOW

by **BILL EASTERLING**

Illustrations by **MARY BETH OWENS**

LITTLE, BROWN AND COMPANY

Boston NewYork Toronto London

First Edition

Grateful acknowledgment is made to the *Huntsville Times*, in which a version of this
story was first published.

Library of Congress Cataloging-in-Publication Data

Easterling, Bill.
    Prize in the snow / by Bill Easterling ; illustrated by Mary Beth
Owens. — 1st ed.
        p.   cm.
    Summary: A young boy sets out one winter day to become a great
hunter, but when he catches a helpless rabbit, his plans change.
    ISBN 0-316-22489-8
    ISBN 0-316-91158-5 (UK pb)
    [1. Hunting — Fiction. 2. Rabbits — Fiction.] I. Owens, Mary
Beth, ill. II. Title.
PZ7.E12674Pr   1994
[E] — dc20   92-23411

10 9 8 7 6 5 4 3

NIL

Published simultaneously in Canada by Little, Brown & Company Limited
and in Great Britain by Little, Brown and Company (UK) Limited
Printed in Italy

For Leigh and Mike, from their grateful father

— B. E.

For Sam

— M. B. O.

There was that peculiar crunching sound as the boy's
booted feet plunged into the whiteness of the snow. A cold
February wind was blowing through the pines. The wind made
a mournful sound.

He was not afraid. Rather he had feelings he had never tasted before. His throat was tight, his stomach knotted. He carried under his arm a wooden box, and in his pocket a stick and a carrot. A long string was tied to the stick.

This was the day he planned to become a great hunter.
He had watched the older boys for a week, and he knew that
he, too, could catch a rabbit or a bird. It was easy.

He had his brother's box and stick. The carrot came from his refrigerator. Now he was deep in the pine thicket near his house and there was no turning back. His heart was beating rapidly.

He chose a small clearing to put the trap in. All you had to
do was set the box on the ground, prop it up with the stick, lay
the carrot under it. Then when the rabbit or bird came, pull the
string. Just like that.

When it was ready he hid behind a tree.

It took a long time. He was about to give up.

And then he saw the rabbit. It came hopping slowly out of
a pile of brush, sniffing, desperately searching for food. It was
deep winter, and there was nothing left to eat in the forest.
But the boy himself knew nothing of hunger. He held his breath
as he watched, hoping almost aloud that the rabbit would
take his bait.

Then the rabbit saw the carrot and dove for the box.

The boy could not keep from yelling aloud as he jerked the
string. The box fell with a thud on the snow.

For a moment the boy just stood there, stunned.

Then he slowly made his way to the box. A dozen thoughts crowded his mind. What should he do next? When the older boys lifted the box the rabbit ran or the bird flew. He did not want to lose his rabbit. He wanted to take it home and show it off. His brother and the older boys would laugh at him if he didn't have it to show.

Cautiously he knelt down to lift the box. Do rabbits bite? Do they have teeth? Will it hurt? It didn't matter. He had to have it.

But the rabbit didn't move. It stood stock-still with a
desperate and doomed look in its eyes. The boy knew
something was wrong. Instead of finding a prize to be taken
home, he saw a skeleton covered with fur. The rabbit could not
run, for it was starving and near death.

The boy took away the box and the stick. He put the carrot right in front of the rabbit's nose. Still the rabbit did not move, nor did it take its eyes off the boy.

Then the boy hid behind the tree. And in a moment the
rabbit began to nibble on the carrot. When the rabbit was full,
it hopped slowly off toward the brush pile and disappeared.

The boy came from behind the tree and walked over to the carrot. He picked it up, took it over to the brush pile, and laid it down right by where the rabbit had disappeared. Then he straightened up and stood there for a long moment. Through the pines he could see the lights coming on inside his house. He started for home.

"I'll bring it some bread tomorrow," he thought as his boots broke through the crusty snow.